SECRET HEART OF LACIE BLADE

DIANE J. REED

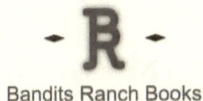

Bandits Ranch Books

This novella is dedicated to all those with big hearts who break the rules in the name of love.

❧ I ❧

The iron grill door slammed behind Lacie Blade with a heavy clang that made her wince. For six hellish months, every time she'd heard that sound echo through Pitchfork Run Correctional Facility, convicts had been entering the prison, not leaving. It was still hard to believe her turn of fortune at being paroled today, especially since she hadn't exactly shown "good behavior." A sweet disposition never helped anyone survive this run-down jailhouse in southern Ohio at the border of Kentucky. But it was so overcrowded that her non-violent drug rap made her a Bambi compared to the homicide offenders she rubbed shoulders with—and sometimes delivered knuckle sandwiches to—on a regular basis.

"Betcha ain't gonna wear orange anytime soon," the warden cracked, handing Lacie a pen to sign out for her purse. She tossed Lacie's former orange jumpsuit into a bin for the next inmate. Lacie avoided her gaze, pressing her hands down her skin-tight black leather coat and skirt to smooth out the wrinkles from being stuffed into a locker all this time. "It's over," she sighed while the warden pushed the button to release the front door. Lacie drew a deep breath and stepped outside, squinting at the slate October sky sliced by occasional rain drops. Finally, she'd head home to Bender Lake and hug her eight-year-old son Winchester so hard he'd squeal from every ounce of love she had bottled up within her.

Half an hour after her cousin Bixby picked her up, Lacie hopped off the back of his vintage Harley onto the soft ground beside Bender Lake. Tears welled in her eyes. She brushed back her ivory hair that fell past her waist and ran—ran till her muscles were ready to melt and her thigh-high boots were caked in mud, but she didn't care. When she reached Granny Tinker's gypsy wagon deep in the woods on the north end of Bender Lake, she didn't bother to knock.

"Winchester!" Lacie swung open the wagon door carved with ornate flourishes. "It's your mom—I'm home!"

Inside the wagon sat Granny Tinker in candlelight, beautiful as always, with her luxurious gray hair cascading to her shoulders and wearing her familiar black velvet dress. She held up an old, leather-bound spell book, pointing to an image of a strange horn surrounded by faded calligraphy. Across from her sat Winchester, utterly mesmerized till he'd heard his mother.

"Mommy!" He sprang from his chair. Lacie wrapped her arms around him and squeezed, cherishing the sparkle in his eyes at the surprise of her return, which she'd made Bixby swear not to tell. Ruffling his wheat-blonde hair, she kneeled to grasp his cheeks.

"Oh, how I've missed you!" Lacie's tears streamed with abandon now. She kissed his forehead, cheeks, and hugged him again for good measure. "I'm home forever, sweetie," she promised. "I'll never leave again. Wait—what's that nasty bruise on your cheek?"

Lacie leaned back, realizing in the dim light that her son had a black eye as well. "Granny!" She shot Granny Tinker a fierce look, who'd been awarded custody of Winchester while she was in the pen because everyone in the county knew her cousin Bixby was too crazy. "What the hell?"

"Now you know perfectly well I'd never smack a child," Granny sniffed. "No matter what he or she done." Her lips curled, revealing the glint of a gold tooth. "'Specially with all these spells for when young'uns get outta line," she winked.

"What happened to you, honey?" Lacie studied Winchester's velvet brown eyes, only to see his gaze dart to the floor.

Granny folded her arms. "Aw, he's been fightin' again. Of all folks, you oughta know what it's like on the playground when one o' your kin is a con."

Lacie's cheeks began to burn.

Oh God—she'd forgotten how cruel the kids at Bender Lake Elementary could be. It was a period in her life she'd sealed into the darkest corners of memory with a stiff lock, refusing to visit the pain for over a decade. Not until this moment did she realize how full circle her life had come—with her baby dealing with the same thing she'd endured over her dad. The shame seared like a branding iron into her heart.

And the mark it left said *Loser*.

"Well, we aren't going to take this lying down," Lacie

vowed, lifting Winchester's chin to make him look her in the eye. "You can bet I'll have a talk with that administration. And when you go back to school tomorrow, I want you to knock that bully flat if he ever dares to touch you again—"

"It warn't a he. Try a *she*," Granny corrected. "That oversized Jenny Coop, whose momma's head of the PTA. I swear they been givin' that girl steroids. But don't you worry," Granny picked up her spell book to scan through the pages, "ever since they expelled Winchester, we ain't had to bother with her none."

"Expelled?" Lacie bolted upright. "My kid's been kicked out of school? Why didn't anyone tell me! For how long?"

"Oh, a couple weeks, I reckon." Granny yawned. She examined a glass jar on her table filled with dried herbs, scrutinizing her inventory for potions. "But it ain't set back Winch none." She unscrewed the top and grabbed a pinch, taking a whiff. "I been homeschooling him myself to make up fer it."

"In what—magic?" Lacie burst, flabbergasted. "That's not going to get my boy into college! For God's sake, Granny, I'll be damned if another Blade's future goes down the tubes." She glanced at the watch on her studded leather wrist cuff. "It's only three-fifteen—I bet the school isn't closed yet. I'm going to swipe my cousin's Harley right now and go have a talk with that principal."

"Mom," Winchester whispered, tugging on his mother's leather coat. "L-Look—"

In that instant, the crystal ball that always sat as a fixture on Granny Tinker's table began to fill with a peculiar lavender haze. Slowly, the cloudiness took on the form of wispy fingers

that swirled into a lazy funnel. When the threads finally
creeped to a halt, they faded into a thin mist. In their wake
surfaced the image of a beating heart.

Bound by a brass lock.

Granny Tinker tilted back her head and cackled as if the
crystal ball had told her a good joke.

"Well now, you do as you see fit," she smiled, gold front
tooth shimmering in the candlelight. She plucked an old, rusty
key from a nearby shelf and held it up to Lacie. "But jes'
remember what them fairy tales I read to you as a girl always
used to say: sometimes banishments are opportunities waitin'
to happen. If'n you don't let 'em pass you by."

Granny set the key on top of her spell book. In the
darkness, Lacie could've sworn she saw it sear an impression
into the leather.

"You'll be back to see me afore you know it. By the way, do
me a big favor when you git to that school."

Lacie hugged Winchester close, rattled by Granny's eerie
key and crystal ball, despite the fact that she'd known her since
childhood and used to help her mix potions.

"W-What's that?" Lacie replied.

"Tell that ol' lake rat I been dyin' to see him."

2

The wheels of the Harley skidded over the school parking lot as Lacie rounded a tight corner and vaulted over a curb, spitting mad. She cut the thundering engine right in front of the main office, looking like she'd been blown in by a biker gang bent on revenge. When secretaries spied her from the window, their eyes grew wide and they thrust the entrance into lockdown with a loud metal click.

Lacie swept back long, windblown strands of hair from her face and slid off the bike with fists clenched, a vision of black-leathered fury. The people inside scurried in panic. One man held up a digital camera to take a shot, like he was ready to turn her in to authorities. Lacie rolled her eyes, grateful that cell phones never seemed to work in this backwoods vortex an hour and a half from any cell tower. The last thing she needed was someone emailing video footage of her to the sheriff that would put him in her face within the hour. Counting to twenty, the way prison anger-management counselors taught her, she resisted the urge to punch through the front door window and haul her ass inside. Instead, she attempted a fake smile and rapped on the door.

The office staff argued loudly about whether to let her in, when a tall, dark-haired man in a brown corduroy blazer stepped into the office. He turned to regard Lacie, making her mouth drop. God as her witness, he was the handsomest man she'd ever seen. His wavy chestnut hair framed his strong cheekbones and jaw to perfection, and his hazel eyes had an extraordinary depth to their warm tones of brown and green. Rather than register alarm at her intrusion, his gaze indicated something else. Something Lacie couldn't quite name.

Déjà vu, maybe?

Abruptly, he froze in place, absorbing her face as though he'd seen her long ago in a dream. Scanning her straight blonde hair, the angle of her nose, the curves of her cheeks and chin, he lingered on her soft brown eyes that matched Winchester's. Lacie blushed while he shook his head, as if to break a spell.

He held up his hand to halt the staff's chatter. Disgruntled, they returned to their seats, and he headed for the entrance.

The lock unclicked.

"M-Ms. Blade?" He swung open the front door.

"Um…yeah," she hesitated, startled that he knew her name. She figured Winchester was the spitting image of her, so maybe he'd put two and two together. "Are you the principal? If so, we need to talk."

Murmurs from the staff filled the air like a swarm of bees.

"Oh my God, how did that woman ever get out of prison?"

"I heard she killed somebody."

"Nah, she got caught cooking meth.

Big surprise with the reputation of her family."

Lacie ignored the gossip and marched past them, making a sharp right to head down the hall to the principal's office. She knew this building like the back of her hand from all the times she and her cousins had been sent to the principal for fighting. Just as she expected, the man followed her. He motioned to a chair before stepping behind his desk to sit down.

"I have a feeling I know the purpose of your visit." He perched his elbows on the desk and folded his hands. His hazel eyes bored into hers without a hint of dismay at her painted-on black leather or her criminal record. "Let me tell you something, Ms. Blade. I don't expel children from Bender Lake Elementary for merely rassling on the playground with too much pent-up energy. Your son Winchester shoved Jenny Coop's head into the dirt and proceeded to knock her senseless. She had to have stitches."

"Did you see his face? She gave him a black eye—"

"It was the *fourth* time, Ms. Blade. And not just with Jenny."

"Kids' remarks can be cruel, Mr., um..."

"Winslow." The man tapped his chipped nameplate on the desk. "Jackson Winslow."

Next to the nameplate, Lacie spotted a picture in a mahogany frame. It was of Jackson accepting a trophy in high school, wearing the classic blue blazer from the Breton Boarding School for Boys in Cincinnati. Sure enough, there was the school's gold insignia embroidered on his chest pocket —she'd recognize it anywhere. Full of privilege and entitlement, Breton boys were notorious for sneaking out and heading to Bender Lake to party on Friday nights toting any illegal substances they could find. Then they crashed their expensive cars into trailer parks or the lake and blamed their skirmishes on the locals, who were left to clean up their messes. Their daddies, of course, always bankrolled them out of any trouble with the law. On a nearby wall, Lacie also spied a brass plaque with *Jackson Winslow* etched in regal script beneath the words *Princeton University*. His award was in social justice, of all things.

Lacie wanted to vomit.

"What is this," she narrowed her eyes, pointing at the plaque, "your flipping Peace Corps stint? A chance to prove you can do a year in the trenches before you accept some golden headmaster job at an elite school? Well I have news for you, Mr. Winslow," Lacie leaned forward, her studded leather bracelet clicking against his desk. "Half the kids here are on welfare. The other half eat rabbit and squirrel because their folks are too proud for assistance. Most of them have relatives in jail at one time or another—just like Winchester. Every single day is a struggle, so they don't need anybody, whether it's Jenny Coop or the Pope, pointing out what they already know is crappy about their lives."

Lacie turned over the Breton photo before it made her so angry she wanted to take a swing.

"If you really want to be a leader," she hissed, "you'll stop bullies from making it intolerable for a kid like Winchester to show his face around here. Because believe me, most of your student body knows *exactly* the kind of pain he feels—"

"Principal Winslow!" A shrill voice cut Lacie off. A gray-haired woman burst into his office with a smoking computer in her hands. She laid it on his desk like a heap of smoldering coal. "This is the last one we had that worked!" she reported, nearly hysterical. "What are we going to do? Bus the kids half an hour away to the county library? We don't even have the money for gas!"

A trickle fell down the woman's cheek, but it wasn't from sweat or tears.

Lacie glanced up at the drops of rain leeching through the ceiling tiles.

Too upset to move, the woman stood her ground, blinking back any moisture that dribbled onto her face. She looked like she was used to it.

Jackson buried his head in his hands. After a pause, he picked up the receiver to a 1970s-style phone and began to punch the number pad, giving off odd melodic tones. The woman wagged her finger.

"Won't do a bit of good to call the head of the PTA for more fundraising," she warned, wiping a few drops from her brow. "Because she just quit. 'Hopeless' I believe is the word she used."

"Patty Coop quit?" Jackson set down the receiver. With a long sigh, he tilted back in his chair and glared at Lacie. The fact that his eyes were so beautiful made her uncomfortable.

"As you can see, Ms. Blade," he pointed out, "no one is more aware than I am about how hard things are at Bender Lake Elementary. And unless you happen to have a magic wand, I suggest you go home to your son, tell him to grow a thicker skin, and teach him to stop beating on other kids. Now if you don't mind, I need to call every county and state resource I can find to ask for more funds—"

"Unless…" Lacie countered with a gleam in her eye.

"Unless what?" he replied, impatient. "I don't mean to cut you short, Ms. Blade. But I have to get a hold of the Department of Education in Columbus before five."

"Can you excuse us for a minute?" Lacie said sweetly to the woman, who'd taken to staring at the growing puddle beside her feet. With a nod, she brushed off the ashy stains from her arms and turned to head down the hall.

Lacie leaped to close the door. A sly smile surfaced on her lips.

"Unless I can get you the cash."

Jackson did a double take.

"W-What are you talking about?"

"Money, for Christ's sake."

Lacie plopped down in her chair and stared the principal in the eye. "*Serious* money. You need funds, and I need my child to go to school. Deal?"

"But I don't see how anyone could possibly…"

Lacie turned a deaf ear to his rationale, enjoying the befuddlement on his face while he kept talking. He was so good looking she found herself wondering what it would be like to run her fingers through his hair, and it was hard not to stare into his striking hazel eyes that flared whenever he got passionate about the school. But what really got to her was the tenderness in his gaze, even when stressed or angered, as if he was always prepared to let lost souls and children into his heart. Lacie shook her head. Don't believe it for a minute, she reminded herself. Every Breton boy you've ever met was a secret sociopath—no different on the inside than cons in the pen. They just come from softer circumstances. He's probably perfected that sensitive look to climb up in the world.

"Maybe it's high time somebody taught you a thing or two about how Bender Lake really operates," Lacie crossed her arms, interrupting Jackson. "Because what we're dealing with here is an underground economy. Trade, swap, barter—that's how folks get along. And pardon my French, but sometimes the real assholes will pony up hefty wads of cash if you know something about them they don't want nobody else to know. Especially the law."

Lacie sat up straight in her chair.

"So here's what I propose: If I manage to get enough, uh...*donations*...to cover a new roof and a computer for every student, then you let Winchester back into school for good. Just give me two weeks, Mr. Winslow, and don't ask any questions." She gazed straight into his eyes that were way too pretty for a grown man's face, let alone anyone's good. "If I fail, the deal's off. You game?"

"A-Are you talking about becoming president of the PTA?"

"If that's what you want to call it. Sure."

Jackson had to brush his hand over his mouth to hide his smirk.

Lacie couldn't help noticing the twinkle in his eyes. It made him even more handsome than before, especially when he attempted to stifle the full-on laughter that was bubbling up inside.

"Oh Ms. Blade," he swallowed down a chuckle, "imagine the hue and cry I'd have to deal with at the superintendent's office if I allowed the head of the PTA to be somebody who, um, you know——"

"Served time?"

Lacie fell silent.

But the shame that seared through her heart felt like an electric scream.

Without a word, she reached for her purse.

To her surprise, Jackson's eyes arrested hers, registering the deep pain from her prison experience that was still too raw. All at once, he seemed vulnerable, like Winchester—someone who knew the humiliation and abandonment of losing a loved one to the system, who'd been forced to navigate the rollercoaster of courts and sentencing. And who'd learned the hard way that soul resignation was the only way to survive.

Jackson grasped her hand. His palm felt warm and comforting.

"I-I'm so sorry, Ms. Blade. What a thoughtless thing for me to say."

Lacie nodded, wishing she could surrender for a moment, but she yanked back her hand. This man's pity felt both good and horrible at the same time, like a street drug she had no business messing with. She couldn't decide whether to thank him or deck him. What would a trust-fund, former prep-boy like him know about the hell she'd just been through? And had he ever considered the term "falsely convicted"?

"I *don't* cook meth," she blurted in a low tone full of venom. "Let's get one thing straight: I love Winchester more than my own life. And I don't give a damn how many times you've heard this from cons—I didn't do it. I was making *candy*, Mr. Winslow."

Lacie's cheeks simmered, body trembling, but she couldn't stop spilling the truth.

"I was trying to cook peanut brittle to sell at the Moo N' Brew Drive Thru for extra cash beyond my shift with Jed's 24-hour Tow Trucks. My crummy gas stove blew up. They found me unconscious ten feet from the carcass of my trailer."

Lacie pushed up her leather coat sleeves to reveal the burn scars.

"When the fire department came, they found money scattered everywhere. Ten thousand bucks my asshole ex-boyfriend apparently stuffed under my mattress before he got arrested a year ago. I had no idea—the locks didn't work on my trailer anymore. Law enforcement assumed I'd been running a meth lab. It didn't help that the sheriff had the hots for me and decided to get even after I'd refused to go to his place."

Lacie shook her head, blinking back tears.

"You'd think investigators could tell the goddamn difference between chemicals and sugar compounds. And why, oh why, wouldn't I have spent that ten grand on a better trailer with good locks if I'd known I had it? But Judge Bent and the sheriff are buddies, so he decided to make a quick example of me with the false evidence the sheriff planted. Let's just say I couldn't afford the highest quality lawyers."

Lacie's hands had balled into fists. She rolled down her sleeves and stood up to leave.

"We're never going to breathe a word of this again," she

warned. "Got that? There are only two things you need to know."

She held up a finger.

"One: I will do whatever it takes to secure my boy's future."

She held up another finger.

"And two: if that means bringing in a lake-load of money for the PTA, so be it."

Lacie stole a glance at the wall.

"So you can take down your Princeton plaque and hug it inside your fancy house tonight and chew on that for a while."

Lacie swiveled to march to the door, her thigh-high boot heels clicking against the hard tiles.

"I don't have to," Jackson called after her.

Lacie halted. Refusing to turn, she held her breath, bracing for the inevitable dismissal.

"'Cause what happens in Bender Lake has always stayed in Bender Lake," Jackson said. "And as long as you don't target anyone innocent, I won't pry into your business. Just promise me one thing."

"What's that?"

Lacie could practically feel Jackson's gaze drill into her back.

"Keep it legal. Okay? No roughing anybody up. No blackmailing anybody who was just trying to provide for their kids. And Ms. Blade…"

"Yes, Mr. Winslow?"

"Looks like you got yourself a deal."

3

Lacie stretched inside her army canvas sleeping bag and released a yawn. The floorboards of Granny Tinker's wagon took on a soft glow from a lantern, helping her relax after events of the day. By her side, Winchester had already drifted to sleep, gently snoring. No sound on earth could be more beautiful, she thought. Lacie nuzzled against his cheek, treasuring his soft skin and boy smell, the warmth of his body and near-liquid silkiness of his hair. Hopefully soon, she sighed, if I can do more midnight runs for Jed's Tow Trucks, I'll get another trailer.

"How 'bout a wagon?" Granny offered out of the blue. She was sitting on her bed at the other end of the table, picking out acorns to drop inside a suede pouch. "I know folks who make 'em, buy or trade."

Lacie shook her head—that woman was born spooky, and she wasn't likely to change anytime soon. "Then you know what I'm about to ask you, huh?" She sat up in her bag. "I paid a visit to Principal Winslow today. And we cut ourselves a bargain."

"Atta girl!" Granny championed. She hopped down from her bed and pulled the velvet cover off her crystal ball on the table. "Come on up an' let's get crackin'."

How does she already know my plan? Lacie wondered, then discarded the thought, too skittish to go there. She slipped out of her bag and joined Granny, taking measured breaths to try and slow her heartbeat. It never got any easier to approach this woman's uncanny insights, regardless of how often she played in her wagon as a child. For the last six months, Lacie had dealt with drug pushers, murderers, and car thieves, and by now she knew their mind games down pat. But nothing that came out of Granny's mouth—or her crystal ball—was ever predictable.

"All right," Lacie began, shoring up her nerves, "we all know this area's been the dumping ground for every psychopath within a hundred-mile radius for decades. Until now. I'm ready to expose a few skeletons, Granny, whether they come from fancy closets or at the bottom of that lake out there. So I need you to help me to find folks who can, shall we say, *afford* to keep me quiet. All non-traceable cash will go to Bender Lake Elementary, of course. Sure as hell beats holding bake sales, don't you think?"

"Land sakes!" Granny burst into a smile. She gave Lacie a high-five. "How I do love yer style, sweetie. And I ain't talkin' about them thigh-high boots you got in the corner of my wagon. Far as I'm concerned, it's about time we put some o' those haints to rest."

"H-Haints?" Lacie shivered a little. "Are you g-going to conjure ghosts?"

"Why sure! Nothing gets a body to pony up like a phantom on his ass. You ready, honey?"

"Oh God," Lacie buried her head in her hands. "I was hoping you'd just look in the crystal ball and tell me where the skeletons are."

"Well that's part of it, but who do you think is doin' the showin'? Those images in the crystal don't come outta nowhere. Them's spirits that help us out."

"Okay, okay," Lacie drew a deep breath, lifting her eyes to Granny. She'd forgotten how smoky gray they were, like a timberwolf's, with that eerie gold in the middle near the pupil that seemed to see through souls.

Granny placed her long, elegant fingers over her crystal ball. She closed her eyes and began to hum softly. If the moment weren't so eerie, Lacie would have almost been soothed by what sounded like a Celtic lullaby, probably from Granny's Irish tinker ancestors. Without warning, Lacie was jolted by Granny's grip on her wrist, giving her a shake.

"You gotta handle the crystal ball for yourself, darlin'. An' concentrate like you mean it. Don't worry," a slight smile pulled at her lips, "I don't figure it'll bite—as long as you ain't no stranger."

Granny's lack of certainty hardly comforted Lacie. Nevertheless, she braved up and set her fingers on the cool surface of the crystal, closing her eyes and listening to Granny's hum. When her eyes flickered open, she saw a pale lavender haze arise in the ball, the kind she'd seen the day before. Soon, the smoke thickened, then leveled a little to reveal the twinkling lights of a big city. It was the night skyline of Cincinnati.

Granny's gaze narrowed on the image, then at Lacie. "Now that's interesting. Do you recall that case a while back in Cinci of the missing mistress? From Indian Hill, that high falutin' neighborhood? I believe Genevieve was her name."

Lacie rolled her eyes. "I was in prison, Granny."

"Well that poor girl's spirit has been lurking 'round these parts fer months. All kinds o' folks been reporting a woman in white floatin' over the lake at night, an' some have even heard her call out across the water, like she's hoping to be found. Usually I don't poke my nose into such grim affairs, but I expect she'd be grateful fer some closure."

Lacie shifted in her chair, uneasy at the thought. All at once, the city lights in the crystal ball died down. The smoke shifted as if an ethereal hand was opening a broad curtain to expose a farmyard at night, silver tones rimming a barn and fenceposts. Lacie heard several repeated grunts. In the moonlight, she made out the form of a herd of pigs rooting in a corral.

"Wait a second—I'm confused. Weren't you thinking the body might have been dumped in Bender Lake? If that's where people saw a spook?"

Granny shook her head sadly. "Yes ma'am, till I seen this. What a terrible way to go."

"Huh? What do you mean?"

"It's an old trick I ain't seen for decades. A sounder o' hogs can finish off a body in less than an hour, you know."

"Mercy!" Lacie slapped her palm over her mouth. "Are you saying the skeleton's somewhere at a farm?"

"Nope. Them bones got scattered in the lake afterwards —that's why she's here." Granny tapped the crystal ball, which had changed to feature dark water with gentle waves glinting in the moonlight. "What was left of the skeleton, anyway. Them hogs probably polished off at least half the bones."

Lacie choked down a swallow, afraid she might throw up. Suddenly, the last six months in prison didn't seem like the worst fate she could imagine after all. "So what we do now? Try and dredge the lake to find the bones? That could take months—"

Granny's mouth slipped into a smile. "Bake, honey! You said yourself that's what PTA folks do, right? We gotta get cookin'. Lorraine will help—she's the best baker in three counties an' her trailer's just over yonder in Turtle Shores."

Lacie's brows crimped together, baffled

"Sweetheart, t'ain't nobody ever gonna find them bones strewn in the lake, or the law or that rich monster's enemies woulda done so by now. I expect all we gotta do is bake ourselves some Halloween cookies and sell 'em in the right place, an' let Genevieve do the rest. If you know what I mean."

"Uh, I'm not following."

"Oh you will," Granny Tinker cackled. "Trust me, you just git us to that fancy neighborhood in Cincinnati with a table and chairs. Ain't they always having fall festivals this time o' year to throw their money around? Last year I heard Bixby got caught tryin' to sell moonshine at some country club an' got kicked out—but not before he sold four bottles on the sly. We'll just set up our little cookie stand there an' have ourselves a ball." She tapped the crystal with a sparkle in her eye. "A real *crystal* ball."

All at once, the wagon door swung open with a violent bang. Lacie nearly jumped out of her skin. A cold wind swirled around the women, lifting their hair and lingering upon their shoulders with what felt like icy fingers. Lacie shot a glance to Winchester, but her boy remained blissfully asleep, tucked into his bag. Huddling her elbows to make the goosebumps go away, she was afraid to peer at Granny.

"It's all right now, Genevieve," Granny called out in a comforting tone. "We got yer back. An' believe me, that man's gonna pay for what he done. An' pay, an' pay, an' pay—"

In that instant, an odd peace descended on the room, falling upon them like a gentle dew. Lacie wasn't sure, but she thought she smelled the fragrance of rosemary and lavender, laced with some exotic scent she couldn't identify. Granny took a deep sniff and nodded.

"Why, thank you, darlin'," she mentioned to the air, grabbing one of her herb jars from a shelf. "This will do right fine for the cookie recipe." She tucked the jar into a burlap sack that hung beside her on the wall.

"C'mon dearie," she turned to Lacie. "Time fer us to git packin'."

4

Granny's crystal ball looked stark upon the black velvet fabric she and Lacie had draped over their table for a Halloween theme. It was the last Saturday in October, and Lacie had driven them over an hour in her cousin's beat-up truck to Indian Hill Country Club in Cincinnati for their autumn bazaar. All around, the elegant grounds were covered in white canvas tents filled with artisans selling everything from etched wine decanters to original oil paintings.

"Granny," Lacie whispered, watching a woman in an orange linen dress, tailored to her tiny waist, march toward them in matching pumps. "We didn't pay for booth space here —what's the plan if we get caught?"

"Fork up more cookies!" Granny winked, adjusting her crystal ball to make sure it caught the sunlight. "Just tell 'em it's a fundraiser for a nearby backwoods school an' watch how puffed up they git about their station. Rich folks can't feel

uppity unless they have someone to look down on, honey.
Before you know it, there'll be a line at this table hustlin' for
every cookie we got." She held up a black cat frosted on a
sugar cookie and elbowed Lacie, nodding at the woman
charging at them sheathed in orange. "Starting with this piece
o' work."

"Ladies!" the woman called out in a piercing tone. "Our
country club charter specifically forbids tacky costumes and
Halloween decorations. The theme this year is *autumn beauty*.
Not trashy witch wear."

Lacie smirked, amused the woman considered her black
knit minidress with leather thigh boots and Granny's ankle-
length velvet attire any kind of costume. If only she knew the
truth about Granny's other-worldliness, she'd probably run
away screaming.

"Would you like to try a cookie?" Lacie offered. She
plucked a pumpkin-frosted one from a plate to match the
woman's dress. "They're for the Bender Lake Elementary
School fundraiser."

Lacie's hand trembled a little. She wasn't at all sure if the
ghost of Genevieve had followed them to Indian Hill, or what
unearthly magic might be unleashed if the woman took the
cookie. She supposed if she wasn't guilty of anything, nothing
out of the ordinary would occur.

At first the woman shook her head and murmured, "I'm
on a strict, no-sugar diet." But then Granny nudged a cookie
with a bat in black frosting toward her. "They got real vanilla
bean crushed into the recipe, along with a few other secret
ingredients," she mentioned. "Once you take a bite, you'll
never forget the flavor."

"And the first sample's free."

Lacie snatched the cookie from Granny and waved it under the woman's nose.

The woman brooded, weighing their offer, and Lacie could tell she was struggling inside. Lacie had legs up to her armpits and curves that could stop traffic, and she noticed the men scattered across the lawn kept rubbernecking in order to check her out. But she'd never seen an affluent woman in her life who wasn't obsessed about fitting dress sizes that dipped into negative digits.

The rich smell of vanilla and other mysterious ingredients filled the crisp, afternoon air like autumn ambrosia. Before long, the woman caved.

"Oh all right, I suppose I should verify the quality of everything sold here today. One little bite." She grabbed the cookie and nibbled at the edge, surprise widening her eyes. "Oh my gosh, the flavor burst is insane!" She glanced up at the women. "What on earth is in these?"

"Told ya Lorraine was good," Granny whispered to Lacie.

In a blink, the woman wolfed down the entire cookie and was reaching for another. She chewed with the manic determination of a squirrel. "I'm starving!" she confessed, afraid to look them in the eye. "I haven't had anything but diet shakes for three solid weeks. He's having an affair, you know—with my best friend. I mean, my *former* best friend." Hesitantly, she searched Granny's eyes. "I-I just moved out yesterday to a temporary loft in the city. I don't know where to go, what to do with my life. How much are these freaking cookies, anyway? They're the only things that have made me feel good inside for weeks. Better than Prozac—"

Furiously, the woman collected a stack of cookies in her arms to stuff into her purse when Granny gently grasped her shoulder. "I believe you'd be better served by touching my crystal ball, darlin'. After all, sometimes banishments are opportunities waitin' to happen."

Granny shot a glance at Lacie as the woman popped one last cookie into her mouth, clutching her stack of treats to her chest like a life preserver.

"I-I don't know why, but I trust you," she gushed. "I mean, those eyes," she peered into Granny's smoky gray eyes with golden flecks, "surely they see for miles." She reached a quivering hand for the crystal ball and stroked it only once, stepping back as if fearing it might catch on fire. Instantly, a picture arose of her kissing a dark, handsome stranger against the twilight skyline of a European city.

The woman dropped her bundle of cookies to the grass.

"Oh my," she gasped. "You mean Leonard's affair could be the best thing that ever happened to me?" Her gaze flicked from Lacie to Granny. "I've got to tell my friends to get over here! Do you give advice about the stock exchange?"

Lacie shook her head. "Love's the name of our game, sweetie. For a *price*," she quickly added. "Remember, this is a fundraiser—and we do mail order."

"Fantastic!" The woman whipped out a check from her purse and scrawled a thousand dollars and her name, then grabbed as many cookies from the grass as she could hold. "I'll tell all my girlfriends—these cookies work better than our psychiatrists. Andrea! Rebecca!" She dashed across the grounds, ignoring the way her orange pumps teetered as she trotted over the lush grass.

Lacie laughed. "What's in these, Granny? Truth serum? "I'm afraid to try one—"

"I bet they're awesome," a familiar voice interrupted.

Lacie whipped around to see Jackson Winslow hovering beside their table. She rolled her eyes. She should've known he'd be back like a shot at Indian Hill on the weekend, the same neighborhood as the Breton Boarding School for Boys, far from the dingy problems of Bender Lake Elementary. He probably lived in a penthouse around the corner.

"Nice to see you, Granny," he said with a twinkle in his eye. "Up to no good, like usual?"

"C'mere! It's been far too long!" Granny swung her arms around him and hugged Jackson till he laughed. "My, my," she clicked her tongue, "how you do fit in 'round here."

"You two *know* each other?" Lacie's brows creased, astonished.

Granny smiled. "Aw, we go way back—"

"To my first days at Bender Lake Elementary, years ago," Jackson cut in. "When I began teaching fifth grade. Granny gave me awfully good advice about relating to, um, my students."

"You were a teacher?" Embarrassment prickled Lacie's cheeks. She'd pegged him as a hit-and-run administrator who'd be on to better things at the end of nine months. The idea that he'd stuck it out this long shocked her.

"Shore thing. He lives only a stone's throw from the school," Granny piped up. "In fact—"

"I came here for a luncheon to talk to the Indian Hill Rotary about donations," Jackson broke in. He glanced down at his shabby corduroy blazer that nevertheless brought out the brilliant color in his eyes. "Unfortunately, our school has a lot of competition from other charities."

"But our cookies *don't*." Granny's eyes narrowed at the lavender mist filling her crystal ball, only to dissipate and reveal a dark SUV parked beside Bender Lake in moonlight. A shadowy female figure stepped out of the vehicle and threw something into the water.

"Whoa." Lacie cut her eyes to Jackson, wondering if he had a clue what they were really doing, or if Granny's special brand of magic might spook him. "The perp must be nearby, Granny," she whispered. "I didn't factor on it being a woman. Kind of ironic, considering I just left prison where there were swarms of them."

"Sh," Granny cautioned. "Just let them cookies do the talkin'." She clutched the crystal ball and carefully hid it beneath the table.

At that moment, a tall, elegant woman in a brown silk dress accented by tasteful autumn leaves stepped near their stand. "Cookies," she said dryly, brushing back her bobbed auburn hair. "My husband might like them, but he's so picky. He only eats artisanal foods. How much?"

"Depends on how many you buy," Lacie answered with her best poker face, the one she'd acquired in prison whenever she knew a homicide offender was nearby. "Here, try a sample."

She attempted to keep her hand steady as she plucked a cookie with a skeleton depicted in frosting. Although Lacie had met more murderers than she cared to remember, the fact that everything about this woman screamed well-heeled suburban housewife was new. Chewing her lip, she wondered what hell was about to break loose when this woman took a bite.

With a sly look in her eye, Granny replaced her crystal ball on the table as the woman nibbled on the cookie. Her eyes drifted down to the lavender smoke that seeped inside the ball, which slowly separated to reveal Bender Lake. At the shore, a shaft of moonlight glinted off the woman's auburn hair while she stared into the water, throwing in bone after bone. "Goodbye," she called out in a tremulous voice, before burying her face in her hands. Her body became racked in sobs.

The woman stepped back in terror from the table, visibly shaking. On her dress was a name tag with the local garden club insignia that read "Priscilla Cross."

"Well now, Priscilla," Lacie moved in to seal the deal. Her gaze darted to Jackson, whose hazel eyes had narrowed to slits, not at all shocked by Granny's revealing crystal ball. "You can have a whole dozen of these cookies. *If* you're in the mood to be generous."

"Sh-She attacked me!" Priscilla's voice broke. She swallowed awkwardly, appearing to choke back her words, yet her lips trembled with an uncontrollable urge to speak. In desperation, she stuffed two more cookies into her mouth like they might slow her confession, only to gulp them down and babble out of control. "She said she was going to kill me if I didn't leave my husband and run away that night. She had a knife and everything!"

With quivering fingers, Priscilla pushed aside the v-neck collar of her silk dress to reveal a ghastly scar beside her heart. "I-I loved her! Her passion made me feel alive again. I was just afraid—I'd never seen that side of her before. We'd gone to a lovely farm in the country to take a midnight stroll. When she started to argue, she went crazy and sank her knife into my chest. She said we should both kill ourselves and be lovers in heaven. I pushed her back and then passed out. When I came to, I found she'd fallen into the pig pen and must have broken her neck. The hogs had already started to…"

Priscilla covered her mouth, revolted at the memory. Her pale face turned green from the horror. "Y-You don't know what it's like in this city when you're involved in a scandal," she confided with halting breaths. "The media will attack you. They can make you lose everything! People aren't open to, you know, different ideas about—"

"True love?" Granny finished her words. She tenderly patted her crystal ball. "Believe me, that's what tangles most hearts."

"Y-you won't tell anyone, will you?" Priscilla begged, beseeching them with her amber eyes. "I'd be ruined—"

"Damn straight we will."

Lacie pressed her hands to the table, her nose in Priscilla's face. "Let's get one thing clear," she said with the same steel rod up her back that she'd perfected in prison. "Regardless of your trauma and grief, and the fact that this was an accident, someone's family lost a daughter. A sister. Someone they loved dearly. And they deserve closure. Not the total hell of wondering what happened to their relative for the rest of their lives."

"That's right," added Jackson, to Lacie's surprise. He folded his arms in a formidable stance, eyes darkening, indicating he had little pity for Priscilla's cowardice. "When we're through here, we're going to tip off authorities to the whereabouts of your lover's bones. It will be a tough case for investigators, and there probably won't be any of your DNA left on the remnants. But that's the least we can do for the family."

"Besides," Lacie pointed out, glancing at a swirl of mist that arose in the crystal ball, "Genevieve needs that closure, too. You don't want her spirit to haunt you with unfinished business, do you?"

In that instant, a peculiar purple wisp began to lift from the crystal ball, threading higher in the afternoon air like candle smoke. It gently curled around Priscilla, hugging her close. She fluttered her eyes for a moment, as though embraced by an old, familiar lover. Then her eyes became riddled with tears. "I loved you with all my heart!" she whispered. "Oh, Genevieve…my sweet Genevieve…what have we done? I should have gone with you that night! Please don't hold it against me—I was too afraid to tell anyone."

"The Lord forgives, sweetheart," Granny said with sympathetic eyes. "An' so will Genevieve. Don't worry, you'll see her again in the hereafter."

"You r-really think so?" Impulsively, Priscilla leaned forward and gave Granny a hug. When she released her, she wiped away her tears and dove into her purse to pull out a wad of bills featuring the face of Benjamin Franklin. "Here, please take this. For the school children," she gushed in gratitude. "I'll send more later, I promise. Your words are the only thing that have healed my broken heart in months. I'm ready to face whatever happens now, I swear. It's okay if fate deals with me, knowing I'll join Genevieve someday. But just one thing," she pushed aside the plate on the table with trembling fingers. "Please don't give me anymore cookies."

"Much obliged, my dear," Granny nodded, folding the cash and handing it to Lacie. "Jes' remember, you can always come see me again for more healin' at Bender Lake. Last wagon on the left on the north side, by the Turtle Shores Trailer Park."

"But be forewarned," Lacie added. "Never go to Granny unless you're ready to tell the truth. Because nothing on earth can remain hidden from the likes of Granny Tinker."

5

When Lacie turned to Jackson, his face was hardly the picture of victory. Shaking his head, his eyes appeared disturbed by the woman's clandestine behavior as he wrapped Granny's crystal ball in the black velvet and tucked it close to his chest. "Looks like you ladies achieved what you came here for," he remarked, turning to take apart the table. "I bet that woman had no idea she was about to face her darkness. Why am I not surprised, with Granny Tinker around—"

"Wait, if we stay till closing," Lacie butted in, "we could have a computer dipped in gold for every kid. Maybe the school roof, too," she smirked. "Kind of like poker—you gotta know when to hold 'em."

"And when to fold 'em," Jackson replied. "Before folks get suspicious and turn their guns on you—or in this case, their society connections." He sighed and glanced across the perfectly manicured grounds that belied the secrets they'd discovered. "I guess you didn't exactly break laws today, given that it's nearly impossible to prosecute Granny's magic for exposing a guilty conscience. But I'd feel better knowing you two are out of here."

"He's right," confirmed Granny, seizing the ball from Jackson's arm. "We got plenty o' work left to do near Bender Lake with folks we can tap for donations."

"Isn't that like squeezing blood from a stone?" Lacie grabbed an edge of the table to help Jackson fold it. "Bender Lake families are hard up. I'd feel guilty about pestering them."

"Except for Bob," Granny replied. She whipped off the black velvet cover from her crystal ball. Inside the orb was the image of a beer-bellied man with a scruffy beard using a crowbar to break into the school window. After wriggling his wide girth inside, he soon returned with a computer and scurried to hide it in his pickup. Then he went back for more.

"Bob's raiding my office?" Jackson's jaw twisted in fury. "That weasel—those were the only computers we had left! He's already the dirtiest money lender in three states, and now he's gonna fence a poor school's computers? There's a special place in hell for a guy like that."

"And a special place in karma," Granny winked. "You know, those contributions we got today won't do the school a lick o' good if Bob steals all your new computers the minute you git 'em. Looks like it's time to do somethin' about ol' Bob. Tell you what, why don't you ride home on Jackson's motorcycle, an' I'll take Bixby's truck with the folding table. I can drive, you know."

"You've got a motorcycle?" Lacie was startled. She

pictured Jackson as the type to drive a conservative European sedan.

"Only if you promise to wear my helmet," Jackson added.

"An' take these cookies," insisted Granny.

She handed Lacie the last four cookies left. Each one featured a frosted red heart bound by a yellow lock—the same image Lacie had seen in her crystal ball the night before. The sight made her quiver. Slipping the cookies into a bag, she put on her leather jacket and stuffed it inside before she zipped up, only to feel her heart throb against the sack.

And the cookies grew oddly warm.

The fact that she still had Granny's cookies gave Lacie goosebumps as she rode to Bender Lake on the back of Jackson's vintage Cobra that was rusted in several places. While they sped down the highway, she couldn't help wondering what fate might have in store, knowing it wouldn't do any good to call the police on Bob. He'd made so much money ripping off people with sky-high interest on cash loans at his convenience store that he was notorious for buying off the law.

Clutching Jackson tighter around the waist, she marveled at how a prep-school boy like him had ever met Granny? She had to admit, though, it felt good to lean her head against his broad shoulder. His wavy chestnut hair was just long enough to tickle her cheek in the breeze. The sensation and even the smell of his neck seemed familiar in a way that was unnerving. Something about his gentle spirit lingered under her skin like an old friend. Her thoughts were so lost on the reasons he seemed strangely comfortable to her that she lost all sense of time, and she was surprised when his cycle came to a halt near the woods of Bender Lake.

Jackson cut the engine half a mile from *Bob's Beer & Live Bait*, a tacky white building down a lost gravel road with a few letters burnt out from its neon lights. Above the sign was written in red spray paint *QUICK LOANS & PAYCHECKS CASHED*.

"God, I haven't darkened that man's door since I was eight." Lacie removed Jackson's helmet and hung it on the handlebar. "I swear, I'd knock over a bank before I'd ever buy bait or borrow money from that guy."

"I hear ya," Jackson brushed back his windblown hair, making him appear way too good looking for Lacie's equilibrium. He took off his blazer and unraveled his navy tie, then rolled up the sleeves of his blue Oxford shirt. If she didn't know better, Lacie would almost peg him as a country boy. As she expected, he shoved his motorcycle and blazer into a deep pocket of the woods covered in brush and high grass. No one with half a brain ever tipped off Bob to the location of their ride. There were plenty of rumors of folks who got on his bad side who were mysteriously never heard from again, and having a secret getaway vehicle at least leveled the playing field.

"Okay," Jackson took a couple of long strides in the opposite direction of the convenience store. "Let's go."

"Wait, you're headed the wrong way." Lacie grabbed his elbow and pointed at the store.

"Oh, I guarantee he ain't back there," Jackson said with a

rakish smile. Lacie wasn't sure, but she thought she almost heard a boondocks lilt to his voice. "We're headed to Lloyd's junkyard."

Lacie narrowed her eyes. "Wouldn't Bob try to fence the computers at Lucky's Pawn Shop?"

"Not if Lloyd gives better deals for black market electronics," Jackson asserted. To Lacie's surprise, he grabbed her by the hand and pulled her into the shadows of the woods.

"Follow me, and don't ask questions. Remember how you proposed to head the PTA and I gave you free reign? It's the same thing—we're back in Bender Lake now, and we're playing by Bender Lake rules."

Lacie shook her head, puzzled. "How on earth do you know all this stuff?" she demanded. "I thought you were a Breton kid—"

Jackson searched her eyes for a long, awkward moment, as though trying to recover something he'd lost. "Y-you don't remember me do you?" he finally said. He studied the ground and drew a deep breath, then shook his head. "Maybe that's for the best," he concluded. "But I will tell you one thing…"

To Lacie's astonishment, he lifted her knit minidress a few inches and patted the holster on her thigh attached to a black leather garter belt. It held Granny Tinker's pearl-handled pistol she'd named "Fate," which Lacie had swiped before they lit out for Indian Hill, in case there might be trouble.

"If I have anything to do with that gun," Jackson continued, "I could lose my job. And I'm the only principal in the history of Bender Lake Elementary who's stayed longer than sixteen months. I ain't gonna give up on those kids now. Under no circumstances do you pull that pistol from your holster, no matter what happens. Do we have an understanding?"

In that moment, the way Jackson's fierce hazel eyes gazed into Lacie's shook her to the bone. That school meant everything to Jackson, and she felt her heart pound once again against sack of the cookies at her chest. She swallowed hard and gave him a nod.

"Guess it's hard to keep secrets on the back of a motorcycle," Lacie pulled her skirt down. "But if things start to get ugly today, I suggest we give up on confronting Bob." She clutched the holster through her dress. "Or I might have to resort to a little help from Fate."

"Things always get ugly with Bob. But don't worry," Jackson assured her, "I've got a plan. C'mon."

Jackson led her down a backwoods deer path shaded by the canopy of hardwoods. Before long, they reached a clearing on the other side of the lake and a chain-link fence grown over by wild bushes. The grill of an occasional rusted car showed through the tall grass, and nearby was a jack-knifed semi truck turned over on its side. Through the foliage, they heard a deep growl.

"Betty is Lloyd's guard dog," Jackson whispered to Lacie. "Meanest Bluetick Coonhound to ever walk, and if she doesn't like you, she'll rip you to pieces." He scanned the fence carefully, directing Lacie to a spot by the totaled semi truck. "Here," he brushed aside some dirt beneath the fence topped with razor wire, "there's a spot where we can crawl under, if you don't mind kissing the dirt a little. Gimme one of Granny's cookies."

Lacie fished into her coat and handed him one. Jackson

broke it in half, then found a gap in the vines over the fence and held out part of the cookie, meeting the fangs of a snarling pointer the size of a small pony before he yanked back his hand. Instantly, the dog sat down and began to wag. She barked as if expecting another treat.

"Thank God for Granny's potions," Jackson winked. He dropped to the ground and shoved aside more dirt, then crawled through his secret dugout under the fence to the other side, motioning for Lacie to do the same. "What truth you got for me today?" Jackson smiled at Betty, holding up the last half of the cookie for her to beg. She released a gentle yip and he set it on her tongue as Lacie joined him, dusting off her dress.

"Guess this junkyard dog won't be telling no lies," Lacie laughed. She peered through the tall brush and tapped Jackson on the shoulder. Beyond a dented washing machine and a car up on blocks surrounded by foliage walked a lean, sinewy old man. "Lloyd Burns," she whispered. "He must be older than God. I thought he would've passed away by now."

"Too mean to die," Jackson sighed. "I figure we barely beat Bob this afternoon, and he'll be here any minute." He pulled a cell phone from his pocket. "So all we have to do is secretly record this transaction and then get the hell out. Preferably alive."

Sure enough, Bob's old pickup appeared at Lloyd's front gate, and Jackson ducked down and pulled Lacie alongside him to the ground. He pointed through the leaves at a tin-roofed shack, nearly swallowed by honeysuckle. "Lloyd's office," he nodded.

Once again, Jackson grabbed Lacie's hand. Though his palm felt firm and strong, she clutched Granny's bag of cookies at her chest for good measure, where they remained peculiarly warm.

"Please God, or Genevieve, or whoever else is out there that might listen," she whispered under her breath, "keep us safe today. Because Bob sure as hell can be a son of a bitch."

6

By the time Lloyd's gate rolled open and Bob parked his pickup at the ramshackle office to walk inside, Lacie and Jackson had skulked like ninjas through the brush to climb up the back of the shack and hide on the tin roof under a weave of canes and branches. With a quick look at Lacie, Jackson turned on his cell phone video, and Lacie found herself praying he had enough charge to capture good footage. Jackson peered through a hole in the roof and gave Lacie a thumbs up, placing the aperture of his camera over it to record Bob's moves.

"How do, Lloyd. Gotcha more computers today," Bob said. "Three hundred a piece, if you're interested. Cash, of course."

Jackson smiled. "Like I said," he whispered to Lacie, "the junkyard is where the real action is."

"How'd you find out about that secret fence hole?" Lacie pressed, when Jackson put his finger to her lips.

"Well now, let's have ourselves a look," Lloyd replied to Bob. "Why dontcha bring one in?"

Lacie and Jackson heard Bob's footsteps exit the shack, and Lacie found another hole in the roof to spy on him. When Bob returned with a computer in his arms, he was followed by the pointer Betty at his heels.

Bob set the computer on a desk, nervous that the dog was so close, given her vicious reputation. While Lloyd inspected the keyboard and monitor, Betty ignored Bob. She began to sniff frantically, setting her paws on the desk to trace her nose over the computer.

"Everything works, right?" said Lloyd. He plugged in the computer and watched it come alive with the Bender Lake Elementary homepage on the screen. "Geez, I'm surprised they ain't condemned that sad excuse for a school." Lloyd pulled open a drawer to count out cash. He handed the bills to Bob and smiled. "The computer looks fine—an' my Betty sure seems to like it."

At that moment, Betty broke away and tracked a furious line on the dirt floor of the small office as though hot on a trail. She turned over rusty gas and oil cans to reach every corner. Frustrated, she sat up and barked.

"What's gotten into your dog?" Bob stuffed the money into his pocket. "She smell a rabbit or somethin'? You know, we could go huntin' later, if you're up for it—"

Betty interrupted Bob's offer with a long howl. She lifted her paw and pointed her nose at the roof.

"Oh crap!" Lacie whispered to Jackson. "I bet she wants another cookie. I'll throw one past the front of the shack while we split down the back and make a run for it. You ready?"

Lacie unzipped her coat and reached into the paper bag at her chest to pull out another treat. But when she shifted her weight to give it a hurl, the tin roof collapsed. With a loud crash, Lacie and Jackson fell to the floor.

In seconds, Lacie had grabbed Jackson's hand. Without even pausing to see if they'd broken any bones, she yanked him to his feet and darted through the clouds of dust like a woman accustomed to dealing with trouble. Big trouble. Before she got to the door, a blast rang out, and Jackson fell.

"Go!" Jackson cried in an agonized voice. "Don't wait for me!"

"Too late!" Lacie's pistol was already pulled from her thigh holster and aiming at Lloyd's head, who'd emerged from the slowly falling dust. "I'll take you both out right now, Lloyd, if you don't drop that shotgun," she hissed. "Just try me."

"Then it all comes down to who's the faster shot," taunted Lloyd. "What were you two doin' up there, anyway—spying? You won't be the first to meet a watery grave in Bender Lake."

"But we'll be the last to hear you say that," Jackson growled. To Lacie's surprise, he'd grabbed a broken cookie that had fallen to the floor and tossed it to Betty. She gulped it down in one bite, and Jackson motioned to Lloyd. "Get him, girl," he whispered.

In a fury of fur and fangs, Betty flew at Lloyd, knocking him to the ground. Bob pulled out a concealed gun, but Lacie had him pinned in a headlock with her pistol at his temple before he could take a breath. She knocked the gun from his hand with the ease of an expert fighter. God almighty, she thought, at least my time in the pen was good for something.

"Betty!" Jackson called off the dog, holding out the other

hunk of cookie. "You so much as move a muscle," he warned Lloyd, "and I'll send her back at ya." He limped to grab the man's shotgun on the floor and struggled to stand up, leg bleeding from his thigh. "Guess the truth here is that Betty hates that man." Jackson held up the cookie piece and nodded at Lacie. "If Lloyd hadn't made her go hungry all the time, and kicked her whenever she came around, he might not be in this fix right now." He waved the shotgun at the two men. "You fellas get on the floor with your hands behind your heads while my friend goes to get help. Or I promise I'll pump you both with more shot than wild turkeys before Thanksgiving."

"I can hold them off fine," Lacie said, refusing to give up her headlock on Bob. "You told me yourself you could lose your job if the school board hears about you wielding a gun, even in self-defense. Judge Bent's probably in thick with these two."

"Oh I believe you," Jackson smirked. "But as a felon, you could lose your freedom, Lacelle. For good. Nothing's worth separating you from Winchester again."

Lacie began to tremble all over. She slowly dropped her hold on Bob and took a step back.

Lacelle?

No one had called her that name in fifteen years. In fact, no one but her mother and Granny Tinker even knew that was her real name, and that Lacie was just a backwoods nickname her cousins gave her—except for a lonely boy she'd met one summer at the age of twelve. His dad was in jail, just like hers, and they both knew how hard life at Bender Lake could really be. When his dad got released from prison and threatened his aunt, who had custody of him, she and the boy up and disappeared. Rumors claimed they'd changed their names, maybe even moved to another state. They were never heard from again.

"J-J...JJ.?" Lacie stuttered, allowing her pistol to fall to her side. She shook her head in disbelief. "J.J. Winter?"

Jackson clutched his hand over the wound at his thigh and nodded. A trickle of blood seeped between his fingers.

"I don't have much time, Lacelle," he said, holding out a crimson palm for her gun. "Give me your pistol and go get help. Fast."

7

"Told ya banishments are opportunities waitin' to happen," smiled Granny Tinker, shooting a glance at Winchester in a zombie outfit playing corn hole with the other third graders. Her gold front tooth glimmered from the mirror ball that hung over the gym for the Halloween Dance at Bender Lake Elementary. Everyone was wearing a costume except for Granny, who manned a table of cookies for the long line eager to eat them with a cup of bubbling green punch. "Don't you worry none," she assured Lacie, tilting the cookie plate. "These ain't got no secret ingredients. But I do believe that handsome fella over there might like one."

Granny nodded at Jackson, who stood in a dark corner with a cane dressed in rags like Huck Finn. "Oh, how I love it when us lake rats honor our roots." Granny released a long cackle, patting her crystal ball on the table, which appeared to jiggle with shared laughter. When Jackson heard the sound from across the room, his eyes caught Lacie's, and he smiled.

"He does look a bit hungry," Lacie agreed, smoothing the calico fabric of her yellow prairie girl dress that made her look sweet sixteen with her long, ivory-blonde hair, no black leather in sight. "But this time I brought my own." She pulled from her pocket a small package wrapped in foil and unfolded the edges to reveal a carefully preserved cookie. On it was a red heart with a gold lock in frosting. Flashing a smile, she strode across the gym to Jackson.

"Wasn't expecting you to be released in time for the Halloween Dance." Lacie lifted her bonnet to get a better look at him. He appeared paler than when she'd visited him in the hospital yesterday, while he was still under sedation from surgery.

"You weren't expecting me to still have a job," Jackson laughed. "But I guess most folks on the school board have been ripped off by Bob and Lloyd a time or two. And the superintendent reminded them that I'd gotten their deeds on video. They're being held in the county jail."

"Doesn't hurt that you're the only principal who's every stayed, either. Why didn't you tell me?"

"I guess I didn't think you'd be interested in the details of my career—"

"No." Lacie paused, her eyes meeting his. "I mean about being J.J. Winter. You were my best friend that summer. Just before seventh grade, when everything fell apart."

Jackson's face flushed. He shifted his weight with the support of his cane. Then his hazel eyes poured into Lacie's with an intensity that was almost too painful to bear.

"I didn't bring it up because I knew it was the summer that hurt you most. That hurt us both the most. Every day felt like quicksand with our dads in court or prison. Our families were in shambles." He glanced down at her red, lace-up leather boots that matched Granny Tinker's, probably one of her extra pairs. "I thought maybe it was best to give it a rest—you know, that kind of pain."

He spotted the cookie in her hand, his eyes studying the red heart covered with a gold lock.

"I don't need one of Granny's potions to remember the heartache of that summer," Jackson said. "I can tell you the truth straight up: You and Granny were the only people on earth who were kind to me. My aunt and I were poor and desperate, and my dad was a very dangerous man. He was about to be released. I wanted to stay at Bender Lake with all my heart, but…"

Jackson grasped the cookie from Lacie's hand.

"I-I loved you too much to put you in danger."

A tear streamed down Lacie's cheek. Jackson reached up his warm fingers to wipe it away.

"W-Where did you go?" she managed to stutter, blinking back more tears. "I looked for you everywhere. At the lake, in our secret caves, in the meadow where we caught fireflies at twilight. It was like you vanished—like all along, you were just a dream. After that, I had to shut down my heart to deal with reality again—to deal with anything again."

"When my aunt and I skipped town to get away from my dad," Jackson choked up a little, "we hid under aliases in different places for years till she passed away. Then I got sent to a foster home in Cinci. I worked my butt off for that Breton scholarship. You know, so I could—"

He shot a glance around the gym.

"So you could help other kids like you?" Lacie spied Winchester high-fiving his friend after winning a round of corn hole. They moved to Pin-The-Tail-On-Scaredy-Cat, and Winchester smiled like he was having the time of his life. "Maybe Granny's not the only one with superpowers," Lacie nodded. "You've certainly got a way with lost souls, JJ."

Jackson startled, as though still taken aback by hearing that old name aloud. He grinned like he enjoyed the sound of it rolling off Lacie's tongue. Then he searched her eyes.

"Once upon a time, there was a pretty girl at Bender Lake who could make you feel better by just whispering your name," he said. "She had the most beautiful eyes and silky blonde hair I'd ever seen, and her heart was as raw and fresh as sunrise over the lake. She never held anything back. There were no secrets in her—if she cared about you, she'd fight for you to the ends of the earth, if that's what it took to keep you safe. That girl showed me rivers, caves, where to find snakes, and how to dance at dusk when no one was looking. But most of all, she showed me that some people are good to the core, and you can trust them with the most tender parts of you. To me, she was pure magic."

Lacie could tell Jackson was blinking back tears himself now. "No wonder I beat up all the bullies who tried to make fun of her. I would've done anything for her," he admitted. He scraped off the gold frosting from the cookie in his hand, so all that was left was a vibrant red heart. "That girl's name was Lacelle Whitney Blade. And there were no locks upon her love."

To Lacie's surprise, he nibbled a piece of Granny's cookie

and broke off a hunk to give to her. Drawing a deep breath, she sucked up her courage and took a bite.

All at once, the two of them were beside Bender Lake in the moonlight, like no time had passed at all. The gym had evaporated, and what was once a mirror ball had transformed to a twinkling canopy of stars. They appeared to shimmer above them with fresh hope.

"I *did* look for you, Lacelle," Jackson confessed, cupping her cheeks. "When I graduated from college I scoured Bender Lake for over a month and even consulted Granny. But you know how she is—she just smiled and said everything comes back around in its own way. And the fates weren't about to let me find you till it was the right time. But I want you to know, Lacelle," he paused for a moment to catch the way a ray of moonlight glistened over her hair, "I didn't return to Bender Lake just for the kids. I came for you—"

Lacie pressed her lips to his before he could finish, kissing him with the fervor of a long lost love. She circled her arms around his neck. "Don't you ever leave me gain, J.J." she scolded.

To their surprise, loud claps of thunder broke over the lake, resounding through the forest and interrupting their moment. Only it wasn't due to lightning. When Lacie and Jackson glanced up, they saw the gym once again and a small crowd in Halloween costumes applauding them. Lacie spied her cousin Bixby dressed as a werewolf whistling at her through his fangs and encouraging his buddies to do the same.

Jackson laughed and Lacie blushed, removing herself from their embrace to dip into a mischievous curtsy. She grabbed the cookie from Jackson's hand and carefully wrapped it back into the tin foil she had in her pocket. She cradled it against her chest like something precious.

"This time," she whispered, "our magic's never going to end."

"Not if I have anything to do with it," Jackson smiled, reaching for her hand. "And I'll keep that secret heart of yours safe," he promised. "You won't ever have to lock it again."

He gave Granny Tinker a wave. In return, she lifted a plastic cup of bubbling green punch with a knowing smile on her lips.

"Now c'mon," Jackson squeezed Lacie's fingers with a firm grip like he never intended to let go. "Let's fetch ourselves some of Granny's brew."

ABOUT THE AUTHOR

USA TODAY bestselling author Diane J. Reed writes happily ever afters with a touch of magic that make you believe in the power of love. Her stories feed the soul with outlaws, mavericks, and dreamers who have big hearts under big skies and dare to risk all for those they cherish. Because love is more than a feeling—it's the magic that changes everything.

To get the latest on new releases, sign up for Diane J. Reed's newsletter at dianejreed.com.